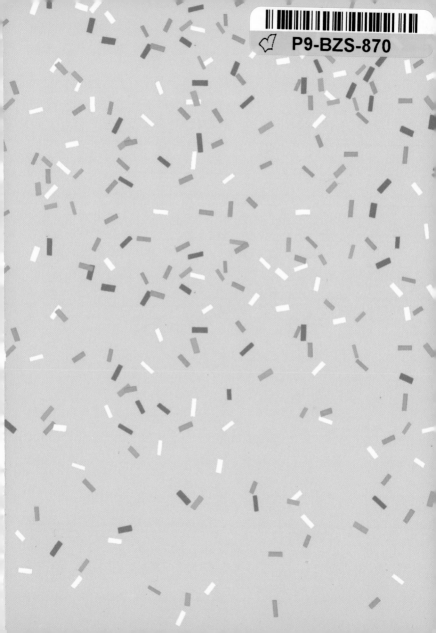

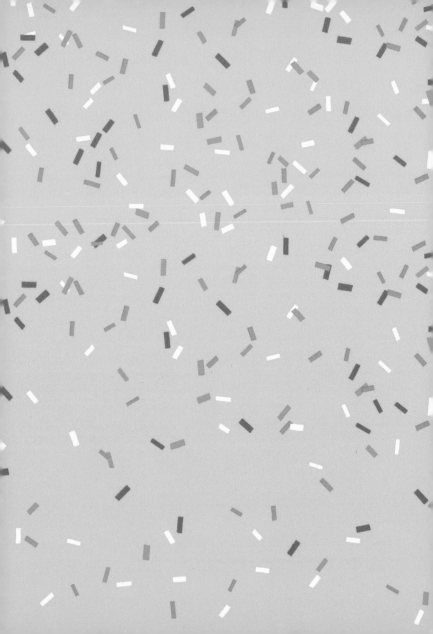

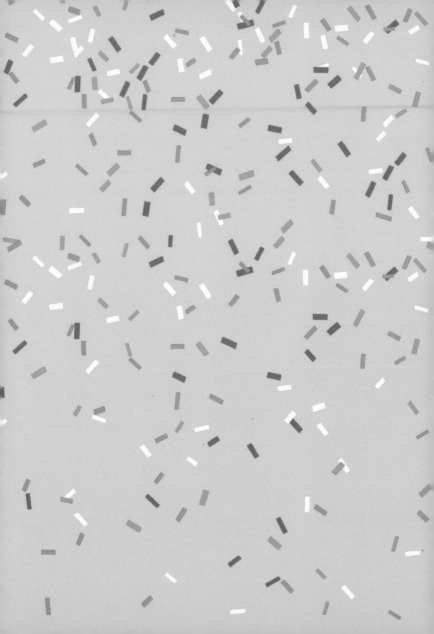

First published in 2017 in Great Britain by
Barrington Stoke Ltd
18 Walker Street, Edinburgh, EH3 7LP

www.barringtonstoke.co.uk

Text © 2017 Jonathan Meres
Illustrations © 2017 Hannah Coulson

A CIP catalogue record for this book is available
from the British Library upon request

ISBN: 978-1-78112-756-8

Printed in China by Leo

This book is in a super readable format for young
readers beginning their independent reading journey.

JONATHAN MERES

Mint Choc Chip at the Market Café

With illustrations by
Hannah Coulson

Barrington Stoke

In memory of Tony's Fabrics
1952–2004

CONTENTS

Chapter 1

To Market, To Market

Priya liked all seven days of the week.

But there were three days she liked best.

In third place was Tuesday. On Tuesday, Priya played football after school. She was goalie because she loved diving for the ball and getting muddy.

Friday was Priya's second best day of the week. On Friday, she went to Science Club and did experiments and learned about Space.

But Saturday was Priya's favourite day of all. On Saturday, she went to the market with her mum and dad and Nana-ji.

Priya's mum and dad had a stall at the market. It was called Sharma's Pet Supplies. It sold food for cats and dogs and other animals. It sold cages for hamsters and gerbils. Bedding for rabbits. Fish tanks and bird seed. Toys and treats. Everything a pet owner might need. Apart from actual pets, that is.

Everyone at the market knew Priya's mum and dad. They knew Nana-ji too. She and Grandpa had started Sharma's Pet Supplies, many years before, when they first arrived from India.

Priya loved to listen to Nana-ji's stories. Best of all she loved the stories of how Nana-ji used to run around the huge markets of Mumbai, when she was a little girl.

But Nana-ji had brothers and sisters to run around with. Not like Priya. Priya was an only child, but that didn't stop her from wandering around the market by herself. That was fine with her mum and dad, as long as she didn't go too far. Because Priya was only nine. Which wasn't very old. But it wasn't very young, either. It was somewhere in the middle.

So, on Saturdays, while Priya's mum and dad were busy serving customers, Priya went exploring. She loved to explore because there were always interesting things to see and hear in the market. Sometimes a new stall might open. Other times, an old stall might close and pull down its shutters for good.

The part of the market that Priya liked best was the part where all the food stalls were. There was so much to see and smell. Shiny, wet fish. The different shapes of fruit and vegetables. Fresh-baked bread that smelled so delicious.

And that's where Priya met Stan, on the day this story started.

Chapter 2
Just Chilling

"Hey, Priya!" a voice called.

Priya turned round. The twins, Daisy and Violet, were walking towards her. Their mum and dad had a market stall, too. It sold flowers. That's why they were called Daisy and Violet.

A boy was with them, but Priya didn't know who he was. She'd never seen him before.

"Hi," said Priya.

"What are you doing?" said Violet, who always wore a bobble hat. Even when it wasn't cold. But that was handy, for Priya. Because the twins looked exactly the same. Without the hat, you couldn't tell who was Violet and who was Daisy.

"Not much," Priya replied. "Just wandering about."

"So you're just chilling?" said Violet.

Priya nodded.

"Cool," said Daisy, who never wore a hat. Even when it was cold. "Let's chill together."

"Good idea," Priya said.

"Oh, this is Stan, by the way," said Violet. "Stan, this is Priya."

"Hi, Stan," said Priya.

"Hi, Priya," said Stan.

So, Priya and Stan and Violet and Daisy all wandered around the market together.

But it was soon time for Violet and Daisy to go back to their mum and dad's stall. They had to help tidy it up and empty all the buckets of water. They didn't mind, because that's how they earned their pocket money.

Chapter 3

When Priya Met Stan

Once the twins had gone, Priya and Stan were left alone together. They weren't sure what to say to each other. After all, they'd only just met.

"What does your name mean?" Stan asked at last.

"My name?" Priya said. "It means 'loved one'."

"That's nice," Stan said.

"Thank you," Priya said. "What does your name mean?"

"Stan?" Stan said.

Priya nodded.

Stan thought for a moment. "I don't think it means anything. It's just short for Stanley."

"Cool," Priya said. "There was a very famous footballer once, called Stanley Matthews. But that was a long, long time ago. When dinosaurs roamed the earth."

Stan laughed. He knew that Priya was joking. Football hadn't even been invented when dinosaurs roamed the earth!

"Do you like football?" Priya asked him.

Stan shook his head. "Not really," he said.

"I do," Priya said. "I play, every Tuesday after …"

But Priya didn't finish what she was saying. She'd just seen something that she'd never seen before.

Another stall that sold pet supplies, like her mum and dad's stall. But this one was called Pete's Pet Supplies.

Priya was puzzled. "That's odd," she said out loud.

But then something even odder happened. The man behind the stall called out, "Oh, there you are, Stan! I thought you'd got lost!"

PETE'S PET SUPPLIES
GRAND OPENING TODAY!
BEST PRICES AROUND!
ONLY THE BEST FOR YOUR FURRY FRIENDS!
PETE & SON LOVE PETS!

"Hi, Dad!" Stan called back.

Priya looked at Stan.

"Wait a minute," she said. "Is that your dad?"

Stan nodded.

"Your mum and dad sell pet supplies?"

"No. Just my dad," Stan said. "I don't have a mum."

"Oh," Priya said. "I'm sorry."

"That's OK," said Stan. "It was a long time ago."

"So, how come I've never seen you before?" Priya said.

"Because I've never been here before," Stan said. "My dad's stall only opened today."

"Well, that explains it then," Priya said.

Stan nodded, again.

"Guess what?" Priya said.

"What?" Stan replied.

"You're never going to believe this."

"Believe what?"

"My mum and dad have a stall that sells pet supplies, too," Priya said.

"Really?" said Stan.

"Yes, really," said Priya. "It's called Sharma's Pet Supplies. It's on the other side of the market."

Stan thought for a moment.

"Cool," he said.

"I know!" Priya laughed. "What a coincidence!"

Chapter 4
Dinosaurs

Priya couldn't wait to tell her mum and dad and Nana-ji the news.

She ran all the way back to their stall to tell them. She told them about how she'd bumped into Daisy and Violet. About how they'd introduced her to a boy called Stan. Which was short for

Stanley. Like Stanley Matthews, the famous old footballer. About how Stan's dad had a market stall that sold pet supplies, too!

"Pardon?" Priya's dad said.

"Did you say ... pet supplies?" Priya's mum said.

"I know!" Priya laughed. "Isn't it funny?"

But Priya's mum and dad didn't laugh. They didn't seem to find it funny at all.

Priya didn't understand. "Don't you think it's an amazing coincidence?" she asked them.

"Yes, Priya. It's a coincidence. But ..."

"But what, Mum?" Priya asked. "What's wrong?"

"Why are we talking to you?" Priya's dad asked.

Priya thought that was a bit of an odd thing to say.

"You always talk to me, Dad!" Priya laughed. "Why wouldn't you talk to me? I'm your daughter!"

"Yes, but why are we talking to you, right NOW?" Priya's dad said.

"Because we don't have any customers," Priya's mum explained, before Priya could answer. "If we were serving customers, we'd be too BUSY to talk to you."

"Look around, Priya," her dad said.

Priya did as her dad said and looked around.

"See how quiet it is?" Priya's dad went on.

Priya nodded. Her dad was right. It was very quiet. There were hardly any people. And there were no customers wanting to buy things from Sharma's Pet Supplies.

"Markets like this are dying!" her mum said.

Priya was alarmed. "Dying?" she said. "Like dinosaurs?"

Priya's dad smiled. Or, at least, he tried to smile. "Yes. A bit like that."

"Everyone's buying things online, these days," Priya's mum said. "Even pet supplies."

"So, the last thing we need is another stall, selling pet supplies," Priya's dad added.

"Oh, I see," Priya said. "I hadn't thought about it like that."

"Now you can maybe understand why your dad and I aren't exactly thrilled?" Priya's mum said.

"But Stan's very nice," Priya said.

"I'm sure he is," said her dad.

Priya looked at her mum and dad for a moment. "So, it's OK for me to see him, then?"

"What do you mean, Priya?" asked Priya's mum.

"Stan and I can still be friends, can't we?"

Priya's dad smiled again. But this time, it was a proper smile. "Of course, you can still be friends!"

Until now, Nana-ji had been sitting at the back of the stall, listening to the conversation. But, all of a sudden, she stood up.

"Follow me, child," she said, and she headed off.

Priya did as she was told and followed Nana-ji. She knew exactly where Nana-ji was going.

And Priya couldn't wait to get there, too!

Chapter 5

The Way the Cookie Crumbles

Priya and Nana-ji sat down in the café. They both ordered their favourite kind of ice cream.

Mint choc chip, with a dollop of chocolate sauce and a chocolate flake, for Priya.

Raspberry ripple, with raspberry sauce and sprinkles, for Nana-ji.

But Priya had a feeling there was another reason why Nana-ji had brought her here. Because Nana-ji always said there was no problem that couldn't be solved by a delicious bowl of ice cream. And that was fine by Priya. Because Priya loved ice cream, too.

"Mmmm," Priya said, tucking in. "This is yummy!"

"Mmmm, yes," Nana-ji agreed. "But not as yummy as my mother's homemade kulfi."

Priya laughed.

"What's so funny, child?" Nana-ji asked, pretending to be cross.

"You always say that, Nana-ji!"

"I'm old," Nana-ji said. "I'm allowed to repeat myself."

Priya tried to picture Nana-ji as a little girl. She pictured Nana-ji running back from school, to help her mother make kulfi. Stirring the milk and sugar and spices in a big pan. Pouring it into little metal cones. And kulfi didn't need any sauce, or sprinkles, because it was already so creamy and sweet.

"Did I ever tell you about the markets, in Mumbai?" Nana-ji asked, interrupting Priya's thoughts.

"About how you used to explore them, with your brothers and sisters?" Priya asked.

"Yes," Nana-ji replied. "But did I ever tell you there were different kinds of markets?"

"What do you mean, Nana-ji?" Priya
wanted to know.

"I mean that some markets sold
only fish," Nana-ji said. "Some sold only
spices. And some sold only beautiful
silks, to make saris that sparkled like
jewels."

Priya listened and nodded. It was very interesting, but why was Nana-ji telling her all this, now?

"It didn't matter that there were lots of stalls that sold fish," Nana-ji said. "It didn't matter that there were lots of stalls that sold spices. Or lots of stalls that sold silks."

Nana-ji looked at Priya for a moment, then she went on talking.

"All competition is good competition, child."

"Pardon?" Priya said, with a frown.

"It gives everyone a kick up the backside."

Priya was shocked. She'd never heard Nana-ji say anything like that before.

Nana-ji smiled when she saw the look on Priya's face. "It's just something people say," she said.

Priya was pleased to hear that. She didn't like the thought of people going around, kicking each other's backsides. It wasn't very polite.

"It doesn't matter if there are two stalls that sell pet supplies," Nana-ji went on. "Or three, or four, or five stalls that sell pet supplies. People will always go where they want to go."

Priya was beginning to understand why Nana-ji was telling her all this.

"It's human nature," Nana-ji said. "It's the way the cookie crumbles."

Priya wasn't sure what that meant. But, like a lot of things that Nana-ji said, it sounded wise and made her feel warm and safe inside.

"But Mum and Dad seem worried," said Priya.

"Everything will be fine, child," Nana-ji said.

Priya looked at Nana-ji. "Promise?"

"I promise." Nana-ji smiled. "Now hurry up and finish your ice cream, before it melts."

Chapter 6

Priya and the Problem

All week, Priya thought about what Nana-ji had said. She still played football on Tuesday, though. And she still went to Science Club on Friday.

But the rest of the time, Priya thought about what Nana-ji had said. About how people go where they want to go. Priya thought that was fine. As long as they wanted to go to Sharma's Pet Supplies, and not Pete's Pet Supplies instead.

It was a big problem. But perhaps there was something Priya could do to help. But what? Make a poster? Hand out some leaflets? Stand with a sign on the end of a stick? What good would any of those things do? Would anybody even see her? After all, she was only nine.

Chapter 7

When Priya Met Stan Again

The next Saturday, Priya was so busy thinking about the big problem that she almost bumped into someone.

"Sorry," she said.

"Sorry," said the person she'd almost bumped into.

It was Stan. "Oh, hi," he said.

"Hi," Priya said.

"I wasn't looking where I was going," said Stan.

"Nor was I," Priya replied.

They looked at each other for a few moments.

"What are you thinking?" Stan said after a while.

"Pardon?" Priya said.

"What are you thinking?" Stan said for a second time.

Priya didn't know what to say. If she told the truth, it might upset Stan. And she didn't want to do that. She didn't know Stan very well, but he was nice. It wasn't his fault that his dad sold pet supplies like Priya's mum and dad. So, she answered his question by not really answering it.

"I'm just thinking about stuff," Priya said.

Stan smiled. "Stuff?" he said.

Priya nodded.

"Cool," Stan said.

They looked at each other for a few more moments.

"Hi, guys!" two voices called at the same time.

Priya and Stan turned around. Daisy and Violet were walking towards them.

"Hi," Priya and Stan said together.

"What are you doing?" said Violet. She had a bobble hat on, as always. But a different one from last week.

"Nothing much," Priya replied.

"Just chilling," Stan added.

"What an amazing coincidence!" said Daisy, who didn't have a hat, as always.

"We're just chilling, too."

Priya smiled. She knew the twins were joking. It wasn't THAT much of a coincidence, at all.

They always saw each other at the
market on Saturdays.

"Want to chill together?" Daisy
asked.

"Sure," Priya said. "Where shall we
go?"

"There's a stall that sells really nice
hats," Violet said. "We could go there, if
you like?"

Daisy laughed. "You and your hats, Violet!"

"I like hats," said Priya.

"Let's go," said Stan.

Chapter 8

A Kick up the Backside

Everything was very quiet when Priya got back to her mum and dad's stall. Even more quiet than normal. But why? That's what Priya wanted to know. And she didn't have to wait very long to find out.

"I'm afraid we've had some bad news," Priya's dad said.

Priya was alarmed. "Oh, my goodness!" she said. "What kind of bad news?"

"They're building a brand-new retail park," her mum said.

"Retail park?" Priya said.

"A shopping centre – on the edge of town," Priya's mum told her. "There will be all kinds of different shops and restaurants. There will be a cinema and a bowling alley, too. And a huge car park. People won't need to go anywhere else. They'll stay there all day."

Priya frowned. 'Why is a retail park such a bad thing?' she thought. In fact, it sounded like a pretty good thing. Especially the cinema and the bowling alley. That sounded like fun!

"And guess what?" Priya's dad said.

"What, Dad?" Priya said.

"One of the shops will be a pet shop."

"Oh," Priya said.

"A great big pet shop," her mum
went on. "A pet shop that sells
everything that we sell. And a lot of
other things too."

"Oh," Priya said, again. "Oh dear."

Now Priya understood why this might be bad news. Now she understood why her mum and dad were quiet. Now Pete's Pet Supplies didn't seem like such a big problem after all.

"It's a disaster," Priya's dad said.

"Yes, it is," Priya's mum said, with a nod of her head.

"Stop it, all of you," Nana-ji said. "Don't be so silly."

"Pardon?" Priya's dad said.

"You call THAT a disaster?" Nana-ji said.

"Well ..."

"Well, nothing," Nana-ji said. "Believe me. A retail park is NOT a disaster."

"But ..." Priya's mum said.

"But, nothing," Nana-ji said. "All competition is good competition."

"Yes," Priya said. "It gives everyone a kick up the backside!"

Priya's mum and dad looked shocked.

"Nana-ji said it!" Priya cried. "It's just something people say!"

"Exactly!" Nana-ji said. "Some people will go to the retail park. Some people will still come to the market. Some people will do both. And that's OK."

"Everything will be fine," Priya said with a grin. "It's the way the cookie crumbles."

"Indeed it is, child," Nana-ji said, as she stood up. "Now, follow me."

Priya did as she was told and followed Nana-ji. Because Priya knew exactly where Nana-ji was going. And she was already thinking how yummy a bowl of her favourite ice cream was going to taste.

Our books are tested
for children and young people by
children and young people.

Thanks to everyone who consulted on
a manuscript for their time and effort in
helping us to make our books better
for our readers.

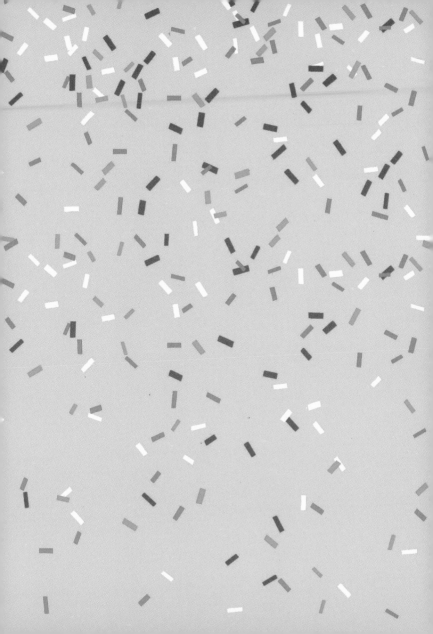

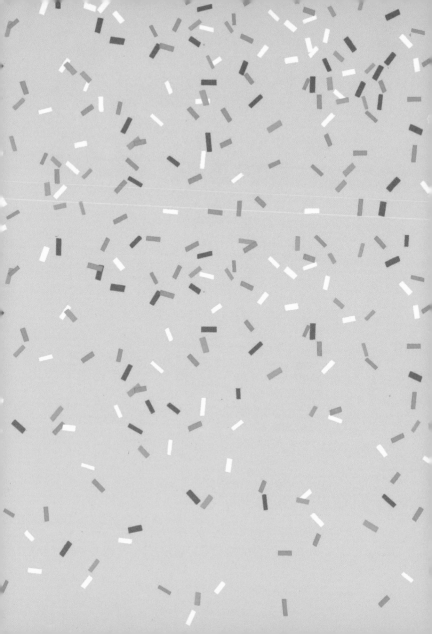